Tilly's Pony Tails

Rosie

the perfect pony

Tilly's Pony Tails
Rosie
the perfect pony

Pippa Funnell

Illustrated by Jennifer Miles

Orion
Children's Books

First published in Great Britain in 2009
by Orion Children's Books
This new edition published in 2012
a division of the Orion Publishing Group Ltd
Orion House
5 Upper St Martin's Lane
London WC2H 9EA
An Hachette UK Company

7 9 10 8 6

A catalogue record for this book is available from the British Library.

ISBN 978 1 84255 711 2

Printed and bound in the UK by
CPI Group (UK) Ltd, Croydon, CR0 4YY

www.orionbooks.co.uk
www.tillysponytails.co.uk

For my good friend,
Antoinette McKeowen

Hello!

When I was little, I, like Tilly, was absolutely crazy about horses and ponies. All my books, pictures and toys had something to do with my four-legged friends.

I was lucky because a great friend of my mother's lent us a little woolly pony called Pepsi. He lived in the field at my best friend's house. I loved spending as much time as possible with him, but hated having to scrape all the mud off his shaggy winter coat. I used to lie in bed at night longing for the day I'd be able to have a smart horse all clipped and snuggled up in a stable with nice warm rugs.

My birthday treat every year was to go to The Horse of the Year Show, and

I remember going to Badminton and Burghley as a child. It was seeing top riders at these famous venues that gave me the inspiration to follow my dreams.

Now I've had the opportunity to ride some wonderful horses, all of whom have a special place in my heart. It's thanks to them that I have achieved my dreams and won so many competitions at the highest level. I still ride all day, every day, live, sleep and breathe horses and I love every minute of it.

Many of you will not be as used to horses as I am, so I have tried to include some of what I have learned in these books. At the back is a glossary so you can look up any unfamiliar words.

I hope you will enjoy reading the books in my series *Tilly's Pony Tails*, as much as I have enjoyed creating a girl who, like me, follows her passions. I hope that Tilly will inspire many readers to follow their dreams.

Love

One

Tilly Redbrow thought she was the luckiest
girl alive. Ever since she was tiny, she had
wanted to ride horses. Now her dreams were
coming true. She spent every minute she
could at Silver Shoe Farm, grooming, feeding
and caring for the horses
there. Tilly had been part
of the Silver Shoe gang
ever since she'd rescued
an abandoned horse
from a busy roadside.

She'd named him Magic Spirit and was his
number one fan. She loved being with him
and she also loved her weekly riding lessons
with Angela, who ran the stables.

The one thing that would make it
perfect, she thought, as she hurried down the
lane to meet her friends, Mia and Cally – the
one thing that would make it all absolutely
perfect would be to have a pony of her own.
Magic Spirit was her dream horse, but he was
a bit too big and still a bit too wild for her. A
patient pony was what she needed.

Tilly found Mia standing outside the
stables, struggling to untangle a hay net.

"Hiya, Tilly," she said. "Do you fancy
watching me practise some jumps today?
Duncan has set up a course in the outdoor
arena."

"Yeah, I'll come along," said Tilly. "But
I've got a lesson with Angela first."

Tilly was learning to ride on Bunny, a
gentle pony who belonged to a girl called
Zoe. She spent a lot of time with her mum in
America, and needed people to exercise and

care for Bunny while she was away.

"Oh dear," said Mia, sounding worried. "Didn't Angela tell you? Zoe got back last night. She's already taken Bunny hacking."

Tilly's heart sank. Now she'd have no pony for her lesson.

"I tell you what," said Mia. "Why don't you take Rosie? I won't be jumping her for a while yet."

Rosie was the pretty strawberry roan that Mia and Cally shared. She was a lovely pony with a gentle temperament.

"Could I?" said Tilly. "That would be great."

"No worries. You'll enjoy riding her. Come on, I'll help you tack up."

Without hesitation, Tilly and Mia collected Rosie and tied her in the yard. Tilly used one of the quick-release knots that Duncan, Angela's head boy, had taught her, while Mia collected the tack from the tack room.

While they were waiting, Tilly stroked Rosie's face and explained:

"I'm going to ride you today, girl. I hope that's okay. I can't wait – Mia and Cally always tell me how lovely you are."

Rosie gently nudged Tilly as if she understood every word.

"Since Rosie's so polite, she only needs a simple eggbutt snaffle," said Mia. "It attaches to this plain leather bridle with a cavesson noseband, and the reins have a rubber grip to stop them slipping through your fingers," she continued.

"Now I need to stand on her left side, called 'the nearside', and put a polypad on her back, which is basically just a numnah with slightly more padding than a plain saddle cloth."

Mia worked steadily as Tilly watched in awe. There was so much to remember! Mia placed the saddle on top of the polypad, taking care to make sure everything was central and that the saddle was correctly placed just behind Rosie's wither. She slid her thumb under the numnah at the front of the saddle and pulled it up, so that there was a gap between Rosie's wither and the numnah.

"Why are you doing that?" asked Tilly.

"To make sure she's comfortable and stop any rubbing on her wither," Mia explained. "Okay, now I'm going over to Rosie's right side, the offside, to attach the girth."

Mia attached the webbing girth to the girth straps under the saddle flap, then moved back to the nearside and gently slid the girth up, trying not to pull too hard.

"It's really important the saddle doesn't slip back, but if it does, you might need a breastplate to keep it in place. Luckily for us, Rosie has quite a tubby tummy, which helps the saddle stay in the correct position!"

Carefully, Mia began to fit the bridle. First, she slipped the reins over Rosie's head, and then placed Rosie's head collar around her neck, in case she tried to get away. While she was doing this, Tilly noticed Mia was holding the bridle in her left hand.

She watched Mia gently place her right arm under Rosie's chin. The pony lowered her head obediently and allowed Mia to hold

her head halfway between her eyes and nose.
Then Mia passed the bridle to her other
hand, so that she was holding both Rosie's
head and bridle in her right hand. She rested
the bit in the palm of her left hand and
gently slid it towards the corner of the pony's
mouth. Rosie opened her mouth obligingly,
and as she took the bit into her mouth, Mia
used her left hand to pull the head piece
over Rosie's ears. Then she freed them with
her fingers so they sat comfortably between
the head piece and browband, helping to
keep the bridle secure.

"Finally we buckle up the throat lash
– there should be space to fit four fingers
between it and Rosie's chin, and next, the
cavesson so it fits snugly just below her
cheekbones. Check that
the bit isn't too low
or too high, and
then we're ready!"
finished Mia.

Phew, thought
Tilly, as she

followed Mia out into the yard. I'm never going to remember all that.

Angela was waiting for them in the yard. She thought Rosie would be a good ride for Tilly too.

"Let's get going then," she said. "You can warm Rosie up for Mia. We're going to do some more work on your trot today. Rosie should make it easy for you."

Tilly mounted and adjusted her position until she found her balance. She sat into the lowest part of the saddle with her hips square. It felt great – Rosie was the perfect size for her.

"Be clear with your leg aid as you ask her to move forward," Angela instructed. "Use your legs and allow her to move forward by softening your arm. I don't want to see too much bouncing today – remember what we said about rising in rhythm to the trot."

Tilly started with a walk, so that she could get used to Rosie's movement.

"That's it. Don't tighten up. Imagine you're a wet noodle – completely relaxed."

Tilly giggled at the idea of being a wet noodle, but it did help her to stay loose.

"Now, when you're ready, give her the cue. Shorten the reins slightly and with a nudge of your legs, ask her to trot. Sit normally for a couple of strides then let her movement send you into a rising trot."

The start of the trot always felt awkward to Tilly. It was as if she was asking different parts of her body to do too many different things. How did Mia and Cally manage to make it look so effortless?

"Feel for the bumps," instructed Angela. "And remember, it's not about strength. Keep your shoulders back, heels down, and knees soft."

As Rosie started to move, Tilly could feel that she had a very easy trot. She was naturally balanced, and was able to trot at a constant speed – not surprising, given what a sweet creature she was. This meant Tilly could rise out of the saddle easily. Suddenly, it all came together and felt very natural.

"Eureka!" cried Angela. "I knew she'd be good for you. Keep it smooth and steady. You've found your rhythm!"

Tilly beamed. It was great to have Angela's encouragement, but already she was thinking about the next challenges. When could she try a canter? When could she try jumping? When could she ride Magic Spirit?

After her lesson, Tilly led Rosie over to the outdoor arena where Mia and Cally were going to be jumping.

"How did it go?" asked Mia, as she took Rosie's reins.

"Good. I've got the hang of my trot – thanks to Rosie."

"She's a fab girl!" grinned Mia, cuddling her pony's shoulder. "She's a mean jumper too. Watch this!"

Mia got started, fearlessly going for the smaller jumps, and building up to the bigger ones. It looked as though she was having the time of her life.

Cally, on the other hand, leaned against the fence, looking unusually glum.

"Are you jumping today?" asked Tilly cheerily. "Rosie's so keen!"

"I suppose so," said Cally reluctantly, as though she wasn't particularly interested. She sounded unhappy. Recently, she'd been missing her sessions at the stables, and she'd taken some days off school as well.

"What's up?" asked Tilly.

"Nothing. Don't worry about me," she muttered, and looked the other way, making it clear that she didn't want to talk.

After clearing several cross poles and a vertical, Mia and Rosie paused and joined them at the fence.

"I love it when it's like this," Mia enthused, patting Rosie's neck and staring up at the blue sky. "Perfect!"

It was one of those brilliant autumn days, when the air is crisp and the sun is bright.

"Are you going to try the oxer?" asked Tilly, glancing over at the biggest obstacle on the far side of the arena. "I can't wait to see you jump it."

"Can't wait to see me crash into it, more like!" chuckled Mia.

Normally Cally laughed at the silly things Mia said, but today there was no response. Tilly could see a sadness in her eyes. They were dull, like Magic Spirit's had been when he'd first arrived 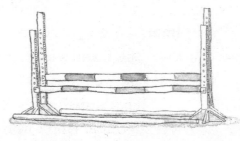 at Silver Shoe Farm as a rescue horse. Tilly had managed to cheer up Magic Spirit, so maybe she could cheer up Cally too. She scooped her arm around Cally's shoulders, and gave her a quick hug.

"I bet you'll jump really well today, Cally. Go for it!"

"Thanks," said Cally, barely moving her lips.

Duncan had arranged five jumps around the arena: two cross poles, two verticals and an ascending oxer. Tilly stared at it and gulped.

"Who's going for that one, then?" Duncan asked.

"Me!" said Mia eagerly, waving her hand about.

"The fearless Mia!" said Duncan, beckoning her forward.

Mia cantered a few circuits of the arena, and when she was ready, lined herself up at the lowest vertical and flew over it.

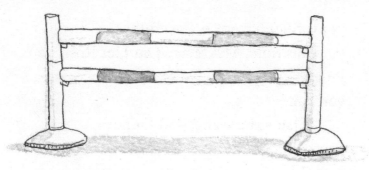

"Effortless!" cooed Duncan.

The next jump Mia tried was the bigger vertical. She cleared it but made a mess of the approach.

"You're panicking too much about Rosie's stride. Try not to interfere. She'll lose her balance if you push her on too fast," explained Duncan.

"But what if she doesn't take off at the right time. I'm worried she'll miss completely!"

"Trust her to work it out for herself," said Duncan firmly. "She knows what she's doing."

Mia and Rosie approached again. Tilly watched closely. She knew she could learn a lot from Duncan, and Rosie was such a great pony. She moved so gracefully.

This time, Mia relaxed and let Rosie judge her own stride. They sailed over the vertical.

"That's the way," said Duncan approvingly. "Why not give the oxer a go now?"

On Mia's first attempt the front pole came down. Duncan hoisted it up, and she tried again. On the second attempt, the pole wobbled but stayed up, and on the third, she cleared it.

Tilly cheered. Cally, who was standing next to her, clapped limply, as though her wrists had no strength in them. She had hardly said a word since Tilly arrived.

"Wow! I can't believe I did that," grinned Mia, as she climbed down from Rosie.

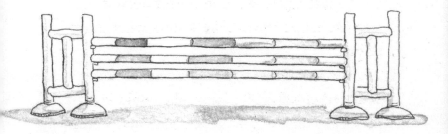

"It felt as though I was flying! Do you want a turn, Cal?"

"No, thanks. I don't really feel like it," whispered Cally, reaching a hand towards Rosie and stroking her nose.

"Something's wrong," said Tilly. "You're not yourself today."

"Oh, it's nothing," sighed Cally.

"I guess you'll tell us when you're ready," said Mia. "I know what you're like."

Cally just shrugged.

Two

When the jumping session had finished, the girls decided to go to the club room and get themselves a snack. Duncan, however, called Tilly over and asked for some help putting the fences together in the centre of the arena.

"I wanted to let you know," he said, as they lifted one of the poles, "that I intend to start working on Magic's training. He's settled in now and he's much more confident about being handled. If you ask me, he's more than ready."

Tilly's stomach somersaulted. She had been hoping for this to happen ever since she'd started riding at Silver Shoe Farm. She shared a special relationship with Magic Spirit, which had begun the moment she'd helped rescue him on the roadside. She was one of the only people he seemed to trust.

"That's brilliant!" she said, smiling and twiddling her horsehair bracelets. One of them contained hairs from Magic Spirit's tail. It matched the original one, which she had worn since she was adopted as a baby.

"You love those bracelets, don't you?" said Duncan, watching her play with them. "And I'm still wearing mine."

He held up his wrist and revealed the bracelet Tilly had made for him, after he'd won the Cosford Hurdle Championship with Red Admiral.

"Are they lucky or something?"

"Maybe," said Tilly.

"They look kind of Native American to me. Come on then, day dreamer," said Duncan, ushering her towards the gate.

"Let's go and see Magic."

"So what are you going to do with him first?" asked Tilly eagerly.

"Well, he's had his health checks – he's been wormed and his feet have been trimmed. His teeth, which were very sharp, have been rasped by Chris Warren, our horse dentist. That's really important – we don't want him to have any pain or discomfort when he tries a bit for the first time."

Tilly listened carefully

"Today, we're going to start lunging, and slowly, as he gets more confident, we'll work on getting him used to different pieces of tack."

"Do you think he'll behave?"

"Well, he's used to being led. It's always important to get the leading relationship right before you do anything else with a horse. So fingers crossed. I could do with some help, though. Would you be up for it?"

Tilly nodded vigorously, thinking there was nothing she'd rather be doing.

In fact, she was so excited about helping Duncan to lunge Magic Spirit she forgot to catch up with Cally and Mia in the club room. When she realised, she sent them a quick text:

GOT TO HELP DUNCAN. SORRY CAN'T MEET U.
LATERS. T X

Then, hoping it would cheer her friend up, she added:

CALLY IS THE BEST! X

Duncan and Tilly dressed in crash hats and gloves and led Magic Spirit to the lunge pen. As they entered the fenced-off area, Duncan explained:

"First, I need you to lead him quietly around the arena, so he gets used to the space. Let's make sure he's happy and not likely to spook at anything before we start the hard work."

Tilly reassured Magic Spirit, stroking his forehead and letting him sniff her horsehair bracelets, then she took the lead rope and told him to walk on. He looked so much healthier than when he had first arrived at Silver Shoe Farm. His neck and quarters were developing muscle and his ribs were now hidden beneath a good layer of fat. His eyes were bright and his coat, which had once been dull and covered in sores, was sleek and clean.

"Stay level with his shoulder," said Duncan, watching closely from the fence.

"Don't drag him – it's not about pulling the horse along. He's got to march himself forward."

Tilly held the lead rope firmly, and walked as though she was trying to get through a crowd, full of determination.

"That's it. You look really confident, Tilly!"

Once Magic Spirit had circled the arena a few times, Duncan showed her how to hold a lunge rein. He looped it neatly so that it wouldn't entangle or trip him up, but there was enough length to create some distance between himself and Magic Spirit.

"The aim," he said, "is to get Magic Spirit to walk or trot an even circle around me. You might have seen it being done in films. Have you ever watched *The Horse Whisperer*?"

"That's my best ever film!" said Tilly, beaming.

"How did I know that, I wonder?" said Duncan, with a wink.

Magic Spirit started to walk the circle, then closed in and tried to return to where Duncan was standing. The lunge line went saggy.

"Ga'an! Move out, boy!" called Duncan, as he flicked the lunge whip with one hand and held the lunge rein with the other, trying to encourage Magic Spirit away from him.

Magic Spirit took the command and stepped out again. He almost completed a circle, then hesitated and tried to return to Duncan again.

Duncan sighed.

"Problem is," he said. "Everything we've encouraged Magic to do so far has involved being close to us, staying by our side. Now we're telling him to go away. Naturally, it's a bit confusing for him."

"I've got an idea," said Tilly, her instincts taking over. "While you're holding the lunge rope, why don't I walk beside him, give him some company until he gets used to circling you at a distance?"

"I don't know," said Duncan. "I can't have you taking any risks . . ."

"Please?" begged Tilly, and before he could argue, she was straightening her crash hat, climbing over the fence and approaching Magic Spirit. He seemed pleased to have her attention and started nuzzling her neck.

"Okay. We'll give it a try," said Duncan, realising he had no choice in the matter.

Sure enough, Magic Spirit managed two complete circles without any difficulty.

"That's great," called Duncan. "It seems to be doing the trick. Now see if you can move away a little."

Tilly praised Magic Spirit and gently stepped back from him.

"Go on, boy!" she said encouragingly. "Walk nicely for Duncan. Good boy!"

To her delight, Magic Spirit did just that. After several turns of lunging on the right rein, Duncan switched sides, and tried lunging on the left. No problems. He even started to break into a canter.

"Wow! Now that he's used to it, he's really keen," said Duncan, impressed. "That was a great idea, Tilly. You gave him the confidence boost he needed – hopefully from now on he'll make fast progress."

Three

School days always went faster when Tilly knew she was going to see the horses in the evening. She was bursting to know how Magic Spirit was doing with his training. It was hard to think about anything else.

Mr Baxter, the History teacher, noticed her daydreaming and was about to tell her off when the bell went.

"At last!" cheered Becky, yawning and stretching. "It's breaktime. I thought that lesson would never end."

Becky was Tilly's closest friend. She wasn't interested in horses at all, but she had got used to the idea of Tilly spending all her time with them, thinking about them, talking about them or reading about them. Secretly, she quite admired her for it.

"What shall we do?" asked Tilly, as they gathered up their books.

"Let's find a bench outside and just chill," said Becky. "You can share my crisps."

They nabbed a bench in the sunniest spot they could find, and sat munching and giggling.

Suddenly, Tilly felt her mobile vibrate. She pulled it from her pocket and checked her inbox. There was a new message from Mia:

WHERE R U? ME'N'CAL R IN THE TOILETS NR THE
ART BLOCK. CAN U GET HERE QUICK!? M X

"What is it?" said Becky, studying Tilly's concerned face.

"I'm not sure," answered Tilly, tapping on her phone.

B THERE AS SOON AS I CAN. WASSUP? T X

Moments later, she got a reply:

CALLY REALLY UPSET. WON'T STOP CRYING.
DUNNO WHAT 2 DO. X

"Oh no," sighed Tilly. "We knew something was bothering Cally the other day at the stables, but she didn't want to talk about it. Now it sounds like she's having a total meltdown."

"We'd better go and find her then," said Becky.

The girls made their way to the Art block, and rushed straight to the girls' toilets. There was Cally, sitting on a toilet seat with the cubicle door open, her head buried in her hands. Mia was trying to comfort her.

"Oh, I'm so glad you're here," she said, turning to Tilly and Becky.

Cally looked up at them. Her eyes were red and puffy.

"I'll get some tissues," said Becky. "You guys have a talk."

Becky was always good in a crisis.

"What's the matter?" said Tilly softly. "We've noticed something's been wrong for days – and we've wanted to help but we need to know what it is first."

Cally wiped her nose and tried to calm her sobs.

"It's . . . it's . . ." she stuttered. "It's my
mum and dad, they're moving house."

Tilly and Mia looked at each other.

"Well, that's quite exciting," said Tilly,
trying to be practical. "Where to?"

"Dubai!"

Tilly and Mia's mouths dropped open.

41

"Dubai!" Mia shrieked. "That's, like, a million, billion miles away! Why on earth are they going there?"

"It's for my dad's work," sniffed Cally. "His company want him to move. It might only be for a few years, but they've made their minds up."

"What about you? What about school? What about . . . Rosie?"

Now Mia's voice was shaking. She looked as though she was about to cry too. She and Cally looked after Rosie together. They shared everything: the grooming, the feeding, the mucking out, and of course, the riding. Without Cally, Mia knew her parents wouldn't be able to afford for her to keep Rosie by herself.

"Oh, you're going to hate me," moaned Cally, burying her head in her hands again.

"Don't be daft," said Tilly. "Why would we hate you? It's not your fault you've got to move."

"You *are* going to hate me," insisted Cally. "Because I'm not moving abroad."

42

Tilly was confused.

"Mum and Dad don't want my studies interrupted, so while they're in Dubai, I'm staying here. I'll visit them in the holidays."

"But that's great," shrugged Mia. "That means we can still see you every day, and we can keep sharing Rosie. My mum'll look after you."

"You don't understand – I'm not staying at Cosford High. They've got me a place at boarding school."

"You mean . . .?" Mia stared at her.

"I'm going to Cavendish Hall," she said. "I had the interview a few weeks ago, and they're buying me my own pony, to keep at the Cavendish Hall stables. We've already been to see him. His name's Mr Fudge."

"That explains why you've been missing riding sessions," said Tilly. "And having days off school."

"Yes, but I've felt so upset and confused, I haven't been able to tell you about it."

"What about Rosie?" said Mia quietly.

"My parents and your parents have been

talking about it. We can't share any more.
I'm really sorry, Mia . . ."

Mia didn't know what to say. She fought
back the tears. Tilly realised she had to step
in and say something. Becky, meanwhile,
passed a pack of tissues around.

"Listen, I'm sure we can work something
out. Cavendish Hall isn't far away. We'll still

see you loads. I've heard their stables are amazing!"

Just then, the bell rang. Time for the next lesson. Seeing that the girls were too upset for school work, Becky made a plan.

"You stay here. I'll make excuses for you."

"Thanks, Becky."

They sat in silence for a moment.

"What we need," said Mia eventually, "is to have a crisis meeting with Angela. She'll know what to do for the best. She always does."

"In the meantime," said Tilly, "tell us about Mr Fudge. What's he like? How big is he?"

Cally's face lit up. She told them how she and her parents had visited several horses and Mr Fudge had been the loveliest. He was a dun Connemara, 15hh – perfect for Cally now that she was growing taller. He was eight years old, and an experienced jumper.

"He sounds gorgeous," said Tilly. "I can't wait to see him. Hey, and when you visit

45

your parents in Dubai, I bet you'll see some amazing racehorses!"

"You'll have to take us with you," said Mia.

"Definitely!" grinned Cally.

Then the three friends hugged for a long time.

Four

That night, Tilly lay awake thinking about Cally's move. It all seemed like such a big change. She knew she had to be cheerful about it for Cally's sake, but she couldn't help feeling sad for Mia and Rosie. They were a gang. Without Cally, it wouldn't be the same. And Mia was bound to be worrying about whether her parents would be able to afford Rosie's upkeep without Cally's support.

Tilly tossed about in her duvet. She

sat up then lay down again. She turned her pillow over and straightened her pyjama legs. But it was no use. She couldn't sleep. She switched on her bedside light and started flicking through old copies of *Pony* magazine to distract herself.

At the back there were always adverts for liveries, riding schools and ponies for sale. One of them said:

Can you help? I'm looking for someone to help share the upkeep and care of Elijah. We are based in Windsor. He is 14.3hh, loves to jump, and would be great for a confident rider. Contact: 08957 349827.

Tilly's mind started to tick. What if she could help take care of Rosie, and share the cost with Mia, like Cally had done? She'd ridden Rosie before so she knew she could handle her. And this way the gang could stay together. Cally could visit them with her new horse, Mr Fudge, whenever she liked.

With a smile, Tilly closed her magazine and switched off the light. Tomorrow morning she would ask her mum and dad if it was possible. Under the duvet she had her fingers crossed.

At breakfast, her brother, Adam, was making a mess with his egg and soldiers. Tilly sat as far away from him as possible and poured herself a bowl of muesli.

"Are you going to Silver Shoe Farm after school, Tilly?" asked her mum.

"'Course. I want to see how Magic Spirit is doing. Duncan's been breaking him in."

"How exciting – that horse has come a long way. Remember what a sorry-looking thing he was when we first found him in the road . . ."

"Also," said Tilly cautiously, "I want to see Mia and Cally and Rosie. Did you know Cally's mum and dad are moving to Dubai?"

"Really?"

"And Cally's going to board at Cavendish Hall so she can finish her school work in this country. And her parents are buying her a new pony . . ."

Tilly's mum raised her eyebrows.

"Which means she won't be able to share Rosie with Mia any more. So I was thinking," said Tilly, pausing to check her mum's reaction, "that maybe, perhaps, I could take her place? Maybe I could share Rosie?"

Mrs Redbrow stared at her daughter and for a moment said nothing, then she brushed her hands down her jeans and smiled in a way that didn't say yes, but it didn't say no either.

"We'll have to talk to your dad, Tilly. Riding lessons are one thing, but actually owning a horse, well, I'm worried it could get quite expensive."

"I'll help," pleaded Tilly. "You can have all my pocket money!"

Tilly's mum smiled and nodded.

"We'll see, Tilly, we'll see . . ."

Five

As soon as the end-of-day bell went, Tilly
ran across the playing fields to meet Mia and
Cally at the school gates. Cally looked a lot
more cheerful. As soon as she saw Tilly, she
smiled and waved.

"Hiya!"

"Are you ready? We don't want to be
late. Angela's having a crisis meeting with us
– she says she's baked some flapjacks."

Tilly was intrigued to find out what
Angela's 'crisis meetings' were like. Angela

was so wise and kind. She was more like a big sister to the girls – she knew everything there was to know about horses, and probably knew about everything else as well.

The girls climbed into Mia's mum's car, and watched the rest of the pupils spilling out of the gates as they pulled away.

"It's gonna be weird when you start boarding at Cavendish Hall, isn't it?" said Mia. "When the bell goes at the end of the day, you won't walk out of the gates, you'll stay in school! You'll be at school all day and all night!"

"It's not like that," said Cally. "There are different things to do in the evenings – it's just that it's all in one place. At least I won't have to go very far to see Mr Fudge. He'll be in the stables at the end of the playing fields. I'm going to ride every morning and evening."

"Sounds perfect to me," Tilly said, smiling.

"When are your parents moving? Your mum and dad did tell me, but it's gone out of my head completely. I've been so busy at the salon," said Mia's mum.

"At the end of the month," said Cally.

Mia gasped.

"That's too soon!"

She folded her arms, and stared moodily out of the window.

"We'd better get an advert out for Rosie then," said Mia's mum. "Let's see if anyone can help us share the upkeep. There must be a few more pony-mad girls like you out there."

"I don't want to share Rosie with any old pony-mad girl," said Mia sulkily.

Tilly was desperate to say something, but she knew she shouldn't get her hopes up until her mum and dad had talked it over. She sat back and tried not to worry about it.

When they reached Silver Shoe Farm, Angela was busy talking to the farrier.

"Give me half an hour, girls," she said. "Then we'll have our meeting. See you in the end barn."

Mia and Cally went to groom Rosie, and Tilly decided to find Duncan and see what progress Magic was making. She was excited by the idea that he might be ready to be backed.

They were in the outdoor arena. It looked as though they'd been working hard. Duncan's blond hair was flopping all over the place. He seemed hot and bothered, and Magic Spirit was pacing restlessly. Tilly was delighted to see how much Magic was starting to build up muscularly as a result of all the training. She was sure this was the start of great things for him.

"How's it going?" called Tilly.

Duncan grumbled something that she couldn't hear.

She watched him attempt to lunge Magic Spirit, but after a few steps Magic shook his head and stopped, then tried to trot in the other direction.

"Whoa, walk!" called Duncan, trying to make the circle smaller by shortening the lunge line.

Magic Spirit slowed a little, but then started to shy. It was as if he didn't want to cooperate.

Eventually the lunge session finished and Duncan came over to Tilly, huffing and puffing.

"Not much progress, I'm afraid. Every little thing seems to agitate him. I've been lunging him for four days. I thought I'd at least be able to get a saddle on him by now."

"But the other day he was doing so well," said Tilly, disappointed.

"I know. It's frustrating. For some reason, since that day, he's gone downhill. I don't know what's changed."

Duncan watched as Magic Spirit walked up to the fence and started to fuss over Tilly, pestering for her attention and affection. Tilly responded by stroking his nose and tickling his ears.

"That's it!" Duncan cried suddenly.

Tilly glanced at him.

"It's you!"

"Me?"

"Magic Spirit only wants to do things
if you're around. The day he did really
well was the day you worked with him.
It happens – horses get picky about who
they work with. You've got such a good

relationship with him, Tilly, it's no surprise he wants your help. You've got the 'Magic' touch!"

Tilly didn't know what to say. She was flattered, but also slightly overwhelmed.

"Let's prove it," said Duncan eagerly. "I'll circle him a few times, and you walk beside him – like you did before. Let's see if he improves."

Tilly pulled on her crash hat, climbed over the fence, and led Magic Spirit into the middle of the arena. Duncan released a length of lunge line and commanded him forward. As if he had been doing it for years, Magic Spirit walked several perfect circles. Even when the line was lengthened, he walked evenly.

Eventually, Duncan commanded him to stop and Magic stood very still, holding his head tall and proud, his neck arched.

"Well done!" said Duncan approvingly. "Good boy! I guess that proves it then!"

Tilly shrugged and smiled.

"If we're going to get Magic Spirit

broken so we can ride him, we're going to have to do it together. Are you up for that, Tilly?"

"Try and stop me," she said, grinning.

Six

Giddy over her triumph with Magic Spirit, Tilly went to meet Angela and the girls in the end barn. They were sitting on hay bales, drinking lemonade and tucking into sticky flapjack slices.

"Have a seat," said Angela, offering Tilly a flapjack. "It sounds like we've got lots to discuss."

They took turns to say what was worrying them about Cally moving to Cavendish Hall, and what they thought they could do about it.

Mia said she was sad that she wouldn't be sharing her pony, Rosie, with Cally any more.

"I know it's hard," said Angela gently. "But things can't stay the same for ever. Before you know it, you'll be too big for Rosie and you'll be selling her and looking for another horse. In the meantime, we'll have to find someone to help you share the cost and effort of keeping her. I'll ask around the stables."

Tilly was sure she noticed Angela give her a look. She wanted to say something, to let them know that she would love to share Rosie with Mia. It was the perfect solution, but she knew she had to wait for her parents to agree to it – and knowing them, that could take ages.

"I'm worried that when I move schools I won't get to see any of you any more," said Cally. "We might all drift apart."

"Well, in that case, we'll have to organise lots of riding trips and events with Cavendish Hall – that way we can see each other regularly," said Angela. "We can go hacking together and maybe have a few outings. How about the cinema or the leisure centre? And of course, we'll always be meeting up at competitions."

The girls agreed this sounded sensible.

But Cally was still worried.

"I can't believe I'll be starting boarding school in a few weeks' time. It's too new and weird."

"I've got an idea," said Angela, sipping her lemonade. "Why don't you take Mia and Tilly along for a visit? If they're with you it might help you to relax and get used to the place. Ask your parents and see what they think."

"That sounds like a plan!' said Mia.

"Let's do it!" added Tilly eagerly.

She had always been curious to see what Cavendish Hall looked like from the inside.

That evening,
it was pizza
night in the
Redbrow
household.
They all sat
at the table,
enjoying pepperoni
and four cheese feasts. Scruff hovered at
their feet, waiting for the crusts.

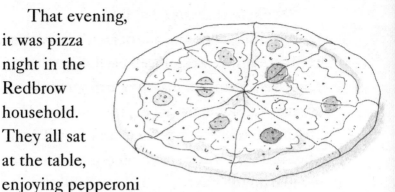

While everyone was quiet, it seemed
like a good time to ask the big question.
Tilly swung her legs backwards and forwards
nervously.

"Ahem," she said, clearing her throat
and pausing nervously. "So,
have you decided whether
I'll be able to share
Rosie or not?
Mia's mum
is putting an
advert out
today you
know."

She flashed them a hopeful grin.

"Oh, to be honest, Tiger Lil', it's been so hectic with the start of term and everything, your mum and I haven't had a chance to discuss it," said her dad.

"We'll talk about it this week," said Mrs Redbrow. "Promise."

She got up from the table to refill the water jug, which made it clear that that was all she would say on the matter.

"Okay," Tilly sighed, deflated.

Why did it seem as if she was always waiting for adults to make decisions? If it were up to her, she would have said yes immediately. When it came to horses, there was no need for discussion and debate. They were the most important things in the world, and that was that.

Seven

Next day, Cally phoned to say that her mum and dad thought it was a good idea for the girls to visit Cavendish Hall together. They suggested they went that afternoon.

Tilly and Mia met Cally at her house. The house itself was almost empty – where sofas and tables had once been, there were piles of cardboard boxes and packing cases. Cally's mum was running up and down the stairs, looking very stressed.

"There's just so much to do!" she said

several times, to anyone who got in her way.

Cally showed the girls her bedroom. It was also empty, except for a mattress and a huge poster of a black stallion.

"I can't bear to take it down yet. It's my favourite one. I used to have pictures and rosettes all over the walls."

"Just like me," said Tilly, smiling.

"Will you have your own room at Cavendish Hall?" asked Mia.

"I'll be sharing with four other girls. Apparently they have ponies as well."

"Cool," said Mia. "It'll be like Pony Club Camp. You can go riding together and have midnight feasts! In that case, I wish I was boarding at Cavendish Hall too!"

At half past two, Cally's dad dropped the girls off at the huge iron gates of Cavendish Hall. They had to press a buzzer, until eventually a voice over the intercom told

them that the gates would be released and
someone would meet them at the reception
area.

The gates began to creak forward.

"It's so grand!" giggled Mia. "It's more
like a country club than a school. I wonder
what the school dinners are like."

"Tastier than the ones we have at
Cosford High, I bet!" said Tilly.

They walked arm in arm up the long
gravel driveway, until they reached the
entrance to the main school building.

"Which way are the stables?" whispered
Tilly, her mind focused on one thing only.

"They're at the end of the playing fields," said Cally. "I'll show you later."

"Hi, girls!" said a friendly voice. They turned to see a sixth form girl waiting for them on the steps.

"My name's Rebecca. I've been asked to show you round. Which one of you is coming to join us then?"

"Me," said Cally. "I'm starting in a few weeks."

"Cool. Welcome to Cavendish Hall. Let's begin the tour."

Rebecca led them through the reception area and into a vast square courtyard. Its walls were covered in plaques and certificates; it had a black-and-white tiled floor, and in the centre, there was a fountain. The sound of the water echoed around the space.

"That's where all the offices are. In front of us is the Maths

department, and over there is English and Drama," Rebecca explained. "The building used to be a manor house, and this courtyard is where the horses and carriages would unload. Apparently, when it's a full moon, you can hear the sound of ghostly horse hooves!"

Mia nudged her friends in the ribs, but Tilly was distracted by the sight of three huge glass cabinets. Each one contained sporting trophies and medals. She wondered how many of them were for show jumping and eventing.

"If we go through here," said Rebecca, pointing to a large archway, "I'll take you to the Great Hall. That's where we have assemblies, plays and presentation evenings. There might be band rehearsals going on at the moment – let's have a look."

Tilly pictured a school orchestra sitting in stiff, formal rows, playing marching band music. But as they approached, she could hear the sound of drums and electric guitars.

"They sound good," she said, with surprise.

"Yeah. They're our school band," explained Rebecca, leading the way through an oak door. The sound of the instruments suddenly became very loud.

"They're called The DropKicks. We can watch them for a bit, if you like."

The girls climbed between the rows of seating and settled themselves. They stared at the stage.

There were three tall young men, swaying about with guitars strapped over their shoulders. At the back, a fourth sat behind a drum kit. Suddenly he came to life with an impressive solo.

"Who's that?" sighed Mia.

"He's amazing," agreed Cally.

"His name is Brook Ashton-Smith," said Rebecca. "He's our head of year. He's not only a good musician, but he's a great rider as well. If you're into horses, he's definitely one to look out for."

Tilly nodded. Maybe he'd won some of the trophies in the cabinet.

"He's so hot!" exclaimed Mia.

"Do you know him then?" asked Cally, grinning at Rebecca. "Can you give us the gossip?"

"Yes, I know him," replied Rebecca crisply. "He's my boyfriend!"

"Oh!" said the three girls together, their faces turning bright red. Then everyone, including Rebecca, fell about laughing.

After the band finished rehearsing, Brook
came over to say hello.

"So, Cally, isn't it? You're joining us at
Cavendish Hall," he said. "You'll love it here.
Have you been down to the stables yet?"

"We were just about to go and see them
now," said Rebecca.

"I'll come down with you then," said Brook. "I've got to go and check on my horse, Solo. He's been a bit tricky recently."

"In that case," squeaked Mia. "Meet Tilly Redbrow."

Mia nudged Tilly forward.

"She's amazing. She's got a special gift for communicating with horses. She could sort your horse out for you."

"Like a horse whisperer?" said Brook, impressed.

"Exactly," said Mia.

"Wow." He smiled at Tilly, and then walked ahead.

"Why did you say all that?" hissed Tilly, blushing with embarrassment.

"I thought it would get his attention," argued Mia. "And it did, didn't it? He might ask for your help."

"But—"

"He's good looking and he's a really nice person," gushed Cally. "What more could we want?"

As they made their way down to the stables, Brook slowed and walked alongside Tilly.

"I'm intrigued by what your friend said," he said, smiling.

"Oh, it's nothing really. Don't listen to her. She's just got a big mouth," said Tilly, staring at her feet.

"No, really, I'm interested. I like to think I've got a special way of communicating with horses myself," he said. "But, well, it's nothing to brag about. It sounds like you've got a real gift. I was wondering whether you could give me a hand."

"I-I suppose I can try," said Tilly. "What's the problem?"

"It's my horse, Solo. He's lost his confidence over the last few days. It's not like him at all, and I can't work out what the problem is. I've been trying to train for a big hunter trials – a cross country competition – but he's reluctant to do the simplest of jumps."

"I can have a look," said Tilly, secretly twiddling her horsehair bracelets between her fingers. "But I don't know if I can make a difference."

"Worth a try," said Brook. "So tell me a bit about yourself. When did you first get involved with horses?"

Tilly explained all about Magic Spirit, and how she had a special relationship with him, and how she had helped Red Admiral win his big race. She didn't mention her horsehair bracelets though, in case it sounded silly.

Meanwhile, several steps ahead of them, Mia, Cally and Rebecca chatted away.

"It's strange," said Rebecca. "But those two seem so lost in their conversation, it's as if they've known each other for years."

Eight

Solo was out in the field. He was a
magnificent animal – a tall thoroughbred with
a silky black coat. He looked like the kind of
horse who wasn't afraid of anything. As soon
as he saw Brook, he came towards him.

"Hello, boy. This is Tilly," Brook said.

Tilly reached up and stroked Solo's neck
and shoulder. She could feel the strength in
him.

"Like I said, he's an amazing horse, but
every time I've taken him over to the cross

country field this last week, he's spooked
and gone all timid."

Tilly thought for a minute.

"Why don't we go there now?" she
suggested.

"Now?"

"Not to jump – just to have a look," she
explained.

She patted Solo confidently. She stroked
his face, allowed him to get used to her smell
and to sniff at her horsehair bracelets. Then
she leaned up and whispered in his ear.

"Come and show me what's bothering you, Solo. Let's find out what it is."

He lifted his head and rubbed it against her hands. Then, as if he was responding to her suggestion, started to move forward.

"He's decided to show us the way," said Brook, following after them.

The cross country field was impressive. It was bigger than any Tilly had seen before. A group of students was lining up at the far end with their ponies, ready for lessons.

"Wait, isn't that—?" Tilly began in surprise. She thought she recognised a top event rider with the group.

"Yes," replied Brook. "He comes in regularly to help us out with out cross country."

The students were wearing matching jodhpurs and light blue airtex shirts under their body protectors, which made them look like a professional team.

Solo stopped at the hedge that surrounded the field, and Tilly caught up with him.

"He seems happy so far," she remarked.

"It's when he gets inside it that he starts to fuss," explained Brook.

Tilly knew they couldn't enter the actual field because the lesson was about to start. She stroked Solo and studied his reaction to the scene. It seemed as though he was focusing his attention on the water jump. It had been specially dug out and had different routes through it, little steps in, a log, and various fences on the exit. It looked fairly easy. Hardly something that would cause a horse like Solo to get jittery.

When Tilly mentioned this, Brook explained Solo had always been very bold and never had a problem with water. But when the first rider and pony in the lesson approached the water, Solo lifted his head and shook it, as though the sight of the jump unsettled him.

"What is it?" said Brook, curious.

Tilly didn't reply. She was too busy watching and concentrating.

The rider continued over the rest of the

jumps, and Solo settled. It wasn't until the second rider approached the water, that he lifted his head and spooked again.

"There's definitely something about that water jump that he doesn't like. It's almost as though he's nervous for the other horses going over it."

"It never used to bother him," said Brook, looking puzzled.

"Maybe we need to investigate," said Tilly.

They waited until the lesson finished, then Brook took his shoes and socks off, rolled up his trousers and paddled into the water, taking care how he stepped.

"Can you find anything?" called Tilly.

"No, nothing unusual . . . although – wait a minute!"

Brook was just about to put his full weight on one foot when he felt something. He bent down and pulled out a broken glass bottle.

"I should have guessed – there had to be a reason. Solo must have sensed it.

No wonder he was put off jumping. He must
have known it was here!"

Solo lowered his head to start munching
the grass. His worry had passed. While Brook
went to dispose of the bottle properly, Tilly
continued to pet and reassure him.

"Hopefully that's the problem solved,"
she said quietly. "You're a lovely creature,
Solo. You remind me of Magic Spirit. Maybe
one day you'll compete against one another.
Maybe you'll still be ridden by Brook, and
Magic Spirit will be ridden by me. Wouldn't

that be wonderful?" she whispered, drifting off into a daydream.

"Sorry to interrupt," said Brook. "I just wanted to say thanks for your help. Tell me what your horse whispering secret is!"

"Oh, I didn't really do much. Luckily, thanks to Solo, no other horse was injured. I can't imagine how horrible an injury there could have been if a horse had trodden on that," said Tilly. "It's hardly horse whispering, is it?"

"No," Brook continued, "what's amazing is how Solo has responded to you. He's so

keen and friendly. Normally, he's completely snooty around strangers – not to mention people he knows well. You obviously do have something special."

Tilly blushed. "Well, I hope it's sorted the problem and his confidence improves."

"Fingers crossed."

Eventually, they were joined by Cally, Mia and Rebecca, who came marching across the grass, laughing and chatting.

"Where have you guys been?" Mia demanded. "We've been looking all round the stables and riding school. They've got so much good equipment," she drooled.

"You've missed most of the tour," said Rebecca.

"What's been keeping you?" quizzed Cally.

Brook and Tilly glanced at Solo, then smiled at each other.

"Nothing much," shrugged Brook. "Tilly's just been helping me – we had a bit of tidying up to do."

Nine

On Cally's last day, there was a strange
atmosphere at the stables. Everyone,
including the horses, could sense that she
was preparing to say goodbye.
Even the barn mice
scampered outside, as
though they wanted to
take one last look at her.

Tilly spent the
morning helping Duncan
work on Magic Spirit's

lunge lesson. At last, Duncan had managed to get a saddle on him.

"He looks like a proper tame horse!" Tilly exclaimed with pride.

"Getting there, anyhow," said Duncan. "He's coped well with more and more tack. I've added stirrups to the saddle, and he doesn't seem to mind them swinging about at his sides."

Magic Spirit caught sight of Tilly and side-stepped gracefully, so that he could show off his physique and let her see how good he looked in the brown leather saddle. His manner reminded her of how she'd felt when she wore a pair of jodhpur boots for the first time.

"I want to keep up this progress," explained Duncan, "so the next step is to start leaning over him, which should be fun!"

"Are you scared?" Tilly asked. She'd watched footage of horses being backed on television. Some of them had bucked and reared and thrown their handlers off.

"Not really. Jack Fisher and I have broken lots of horses and we've both been

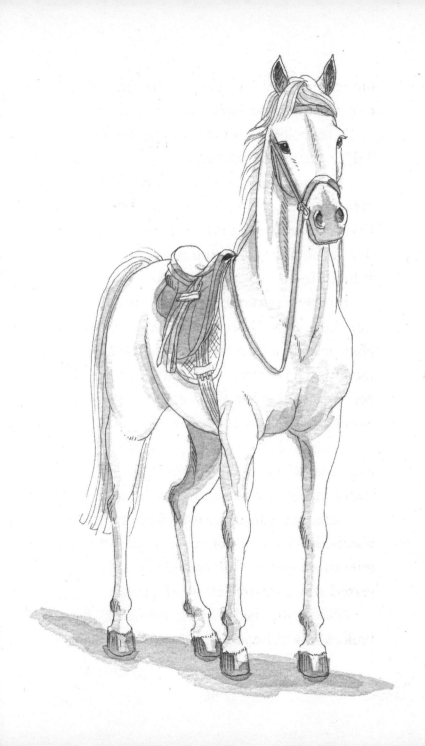

chucked about more times than you've had hot dinners, Tilly! The horse always settles in the end – once it knows we're not giving up."

Tilly watched Magic Spirit peacefully munching the grass. It was hard now to remember the wild, frightened creature he had been when he first arrived at Silver Shoe Farm.

"Do you think he's ready?" she asked.

"Yes. We've built a lot of trust over the last few weeks – which is mostly down to you, Tilly. You helped make the breakthrough. Sometimes I think if anyone should be the first to back Magic Spirit it should be you . . ."

"Can I?" said Tilly, wide-eyed.

Duncan laughed.

"I think your parents would have something to say about that! But don't worry, you'll get your chance eventually."

Duncan began to lunge Magic Spirit around the pen, guiding him forward and using his voice to command Magic to walk, trot and canter. Tilly couldn't help feeling proud of herself at the sight of it. In that instant, she knew that her dream career would be owning her own stables and training young horses. When the lunging was finished she ran off to find Angela and ask her all about it.

"The main thing," Angela explained, as Tilly helped her prepare the evening feeds, "is to get as much experience as you can. Never be afraid to ask questions and listen to advice – that's how you learn."

Tilly nodded.

"Do you think I've got what it takes?"

"Most definitely. Lots of girls and boys come to Silver Shoe Farm wanting to help out and learn to ride – but not everyone sticks with it.

Something tells me you're not going to be one of those!"

"It would help if I had my own horse. Do you know if Mia's found someone to help her with Rosie yet?" Tilly asked cautiously.

"Are you interested?" enquired Angela, smiling. "I know there have been a few replies to the advert, so if you are interested, you'd better get in quick."

"Tell me about it," sighed Tilly. "I'm waiting for my parents to make their minds up."

"Maybe they need a bit of encouragement," said Angela, her eyes twinkling. "Excuse me a minute, Tilly. I've just remembered, I've got to go and make a phone call . . ."

Tilly met Mia and Cally in the club room for a farewell lunch. They made their favourite – cheese sandwiches stuffed with pickled onion crisps.

"Lovely!" said Mia.

"I'm going to miss our lunches together," sighed Cally.

"What about the three of us going for one last hack together this afternoon," suggested Tilly. "I'll see if I can borrow Bunny. Mia can take Aladdin, and Cally, of course, can ride Rosie."

"Let's do it! One last ride!" declared Cally, holding out her hand. The others high-fived her and off they went.

An autumn chill was blowing through the yard, and leaves were scattered everywhere.

"Dress warmly," said Mia. "Winter's on its way."

93

The girls tugged on their fleeces and riding hats and then collected their gear from the tack room. Although they tried hard to be cheerful, a certain sadness hung in the air. It didn't help that Mia kept up a running commentary, saying things like:

"One last tacking up session, one last trot on our favourite forest track . . ."

Eventually, Cally interrupted her.

"It's not like I'm vanishing, you know! I'm only moving to a school down the road!"

The three girls rode out of the yard and headed down the lane, past the hedgerows, over the bridge, and onto the bridlepath. The leaves had turned. It was a spectacular display of red, orange and yellow. As they walked deeper into the forest, the smell of damp moss filled the air. Squirrels hopped between branches, and in the distance, the sound of a woodpecker echoed through the trees.

"I bet there aren't any rides as nice as this at Cavendish Hall," called Mia.

"I bet there are!" responded Cally.

"Aren't!" protested Mia.

"Are!"

"There are lovely tracks everywhere," said Tilly, wondering why the two best friends were so keen to bicker on their last Silver Shoe Farm hack together.

"Anyway, if Cally finds some cool tracks at her new school, she'll take us to them, won't she?"

"Deffo," said Cally.

They trotted on in silence, until they came to a large field.

"Couldn't you just?" said Cally, nodding at the stretch of open land.

"You mean . . .?" grinned Mia.

"Let's do it!" they yelled, and then took off together at a canter, laughing and cheering.

"Wait for me!" said Tilly, using her leg to command Bunny forward. Slowly Bunny advanced into a trot. Tilly was pleased to find that she still had her trotting rhythm, but she didn't catch the others until they'd

stopped at the other side.

"Eek!" said Cally. "Look at the time! My dad's coming in half an hour to help me pack up my stuff. We'd better get back."

"One last canter?" suggested Mia.

"One last," agreed Cally.

The three girls rode back across the field again. Mia and Cally raced ahead, with Tilly behind them. The sooner she could learn to canter the better, she thought to herself.

Ten

Three days later, Tilly got the news she had been hoping to hear.

"We've thought it over, Tiger Lil'," said her dad. "And, well, we've been really impressed by the hard work you've put in at the farm."

"You've certainly shown us how committed you are," added her mum. "So we've talked to Mia's parents and agreed that you can share Rosie – it's all sorted out."

Tilly jumped in the air, then bundled her parents, smothering them with hugs and kisses.

"You're the best ever!" she squealed. "Thank you so much!"

"You might want to thank your friend Angela too – she's very persuasive you know," said her dad quietly.

Tilly just grinned and cuddled Scruff, who was barking at the excitement of it all.

That afternoon, Tilly's dad drove her to Silver Shoe Farm. Instead of dropping her off in the lane as usual, he parked the car and got out.

"Let's see this horse of yours then. I want a complete tour of the stables, Tiger Lil'!"

They approached Rosie's stable, but she wasn't in there.

"Trust us to buy a pony that doesn't exist," said Mr Redbrow.

Tilly groaned at her dad's sense of humour and explained: "She'll be in the long field. She gets turned out most days so that she can graze."

"I see."

They found Rosie enjoying the grass with several other ponies and horses.

"Which one is she?"

"She's the strawberry roan, over there."

"Strawberry roan? Are you sure this is a horse you're describing?"

"Dad!" Tilly declared. "You don't know anything!"

Moments later, Tilly felt a pair of hands grasp her shoulders. It was Mia, sneaking up. The girls faced each other and started hugging and jumping up and down.

"I'm so pleased."

"Me too!"

"We're going to be partners – lucky Rosie!"

"Here," said Mia. "Call her over. Give her this."

She handed Tilly a carrot.

"She loves them. I've got so much to tell you about her."

Tilly held the carrot in the flat of her hand and reached over the fence.

"Rosie!" she called. "Come on, Rosie, girl. Come and say hi."

The carrot gained the attention of all the horses in the field. They walked over inquisitively. A couple started to push forward and aim their noses at Tilly's hand.

Tilly's dad looked slightly nervous.

"They can't jump the fence, can they?"

"Don't worry, Mr Redbrow," said Mia. "They only jump when they see a human they want to eat! Besides, Tilly knows what she's doing."

Tilly pulled back the carrot and shooed the other horses away.

"Sorry guys, this one's for Rosie."

Finally, Rosie came forward to claim her treat. Tilly fussed over her, stroking her forehead and neck.

"You're so beautiful," she cooed. "We're going to have great fun together!"

Tilly and her dad led Rosie back to the yard. "I'll show you how to groom her," said Tilly.

She showed him how to use a curry comb and a body brush, just like Mia and Cally had shown her when she'd first visited the stables. Then she checked Rosie's feet and cleaned her face. Her dad looked on, admiring the affectionate way that Tilly handled her new pony, and helping wherever he could.

As Tilly combed Rosie's tail she collected the loose hair and twisted and plaited it to make one of her horsehair bracelets. She thought about the hairs from her original bracelet. Maybe her real mum had had a special horse too, and that's where they came from. Maybe it was a lucky charm, like Duncan had said.

The next stop was the lunge pen, where Tilly hoped she could show her dad Magic Spirit. To her astonishment, Duncan was in the saddle, struggling a bit but managing to stay on. Jack Fisher was helping.

"It's like cowboy rodeo," said Mr Redbrow. "I reckon I'd be quite good at that!"

They went up to the fence, to see what was happening.

Suddenly Magic Spirit bucked. His head went down, his muscles bunched and his back legs flew out behind him. Duncan couldn't keep his balance.

He was hurled through the air and landed just in front of Tilly and Mr Redbrow. Tilly clasped her hand to her mouth anxiously. Her dad winced.

He was amazed at Magic's strength, and Tilly was too. Although she knew Magic's condition had been steadily improving, she hadn't realised just how strong he was until now.

Thankfully, Duncan didn't seem at all bothered. He calmly picked up the reins and led Magic Spirit over to them.

Tilly introduced him and Jack Fisher to her dad.

"We've met before," said Duncan. "After the races."

"It's the father of our famous little horse whisperer," said Jack Fisher.

"Well, I've heard she's got a way with them," Tilly's dad said, shrugging.

"Just watch this," said Duncan, winking at Tilly.

He whispered something in her ear and Tilly nodded. She reached up to Magic and tickled his neck. She whispered to him and allowed him to sniff her horsehair bracelets.

"Okay, back to work," said Duncan eventually.

Jack Fisher gave him a leg up. This time, Magic Spirit behaved as though he had been ridden all his life. He trotted into the middle of the arena and completed a circuit without a hint of agitation or disobedience.

"Now, he wasn't doing it like that before Tilly showed up," said Jack admiringly.

Mr Redbrow nodded, and Tilly could tell by the expression on his face that he was impressed.

Soon it was time to leave. The sky was beginning to darken. The horses were returning from their rides and being rugged up to shield them from the cold weather. But just as they were saying goodbye, Tilly and her dad noticed a familiar face in the yard. It was Cally. She had ridden over from Cavendish Hall. Tilly rushed over to say hello, and was joined by most of the stable gang. Everyone was keen to meet Cally's handsome new horse, Mr Fudge.

"I told you I'd visit regularly," said Cally, smiling.

"How are you? How's Cavendish Hall?" asked Tilly. She had so many questions, it was hard to know where to begin.

"It's all good,' said Cally. "Everyone's really friendly. I hear you're taking on Rosie. I wanted it to be you more than anyone. How is she?"

"Well, she's definitely missing you, Cally, but she's fine. By the way, I made you this."

Tilly reached into her pocket and handed Cally the horsehair bracelet she had made from Rosie's tail.

"That's so lovely," said Cally.

"It will always remind you of Rosie and it might bring you luck."

"I'll wear it forever."

"And that way you'll always be part of the gang, no matter where you are."

Tilly tied the bracelet around Cally's wrist and briefly held her hand. It seemed as though everything was working out after all.

"Hey, I saw Brook this morning," whispered Cally. "He asked me to pass on a message to you."

Tilly listened.

"He just said, 'Tilly, you're fab, Solo's back on form.'"

Tilly smiled to herself. Everyone kept saying it, and now she was starting to believe it herself – she really did have a special way with horses. She wished she could explain it. She wished she could make sense of it. But for now, she had to be content with simply knowing that she had it.

Pippa's Top Tips

Make sure the head collar is comfortable for your pony. When fitting it, always be careful to avoid their eyes, ears and nose, and don't make it too tight. Head collars are always fitted more loosely than bridles.

Horses can be unpredictable creatures, so you should always take care around them. For example, never loop the lead rope around your hand. If your pony pulls away suddenly, you risk injuring your hand.

Good riding is all about balance and straightness, and the majority of a horse's problems can usually be traced to a rider's poor position.

Always sit tall, as if a piece of string is attached to the top of your head, pulling you up.

Establish a light rein contact. Think of your arm and the rein as a piece of elastic that runs through your hand to your elbow. Your pony can feel the slightest of movements along the rein, so your signals don't need to be over-exaggerated.

A pony's mouth is very sensitive and there's nothing worse than an ill-fitting bit. The bit should be just the right size and position, with the noseband sitting just below the cheek bone.

Hosing your pony's leg can help reduce a swelling if he's taken a knock, but always get a vet to check out any injuries.

Dirty tack can cause skin infections for a horse, so always clean your tack after riding. First, remove any grease and dirt with a hot, damp cloth, then use some saddle soap to keep everything supple.

Careful cleaning also gives you a good chance to check the stitching and see that nothing is damaged or worn out. You should apply a leather dressing to the underside of the tack once a month – but, of course, this won't be necessary for synthetic tack.

Joining your local Pony Club is a great way to learn all the skills you need to care for your horse. They organise rallies and events, and some even run special camps during the school holidays.

Glossary

Hacking (p.11) – Riding in the country for pleasure.

Strawberry Roan (p.11) – A breed of pony with reddish hair mixed with white, hence strawberry.

Quick-release knot (p.11) – A knot used for tying up horses, which, if your horse panics, you can pull the loose end of the rope to release it instantly.

Eggbutt snaffle (p.12) – A type of bit, very commonly used. The egg-shaped rings are fixed to the mouthpiece.

Noseband (p.12) – Part of the bridle that goes around your horse's nose.

Cavesson (p.12) – A type of noseband.

Nearside (p.12) – The left side of a pony.

Offside (p.12) – The right side of a pony.

Numnah (p.12) – Various types of material which go under the saddle to keep the saddle clean and cushion your horse's or pony's back.

Polypad (p.12) – A type of cotton numnah with slightly more padding than a plain saddle cloth.

Wither (p.12) – See points of a horse p 118.

Girth (p.13) – Leather or webbing strap which passes under your horse's stomach and attaches on both sides of the saddle to hold it in place.

Head collar/halter (p.13) – This is used to lead a horse or pony, or tie it up, and usually made of leather or webbing.

Browband (p.15) – Part of the bridle that goes across your horse's forehead.

Throat lash (p.15) – Part of the bridle that runs under your horse's throat and helps to keep the bridle in place.

Cross pole (p.20) – A simple kind of jump made up of two poles crossed with one end of each pole on the ground like an X.

Oxer / parallel (p.21) – Another kind of jump with two vertical poles placed close together.

Vertical (p.22) – A jump with poles or planks placed one directly above another.

Lunging (p.30) – Guiding a horse forward and using your voice to ask him to walk, trot and canter. You stand in the middle and he circles around you on the end of a long rope or lunge line.

Grooming (p.42) – Regular grooming cleans your horse and will prevent any chafing under tack. It keeps your horse healthy and comfortable and will help you form a relationship with him.

Mucking out (p.42) – Your horse or pony's stable needs mucking out once or twice a day, to remove droppings and wet bedding and then replace with fresh bedding.

Connemara (p.45) – A breed of pony (originally Irish) known for its athleticism, versatility and good disposition.

hh / hands (p.45) – A hand is a unit of measurement of equal length to 4 inches or 10.16 cm.

Cross country (p.76) – A cross-country course is designed to test the speed, endurance and jumping ability of the horse – with water features, like ponds and streams, together with different jumps, drops and ditches.

Hunter trials (p.76) – A type of local cross country competition.

Thoroughbred (p.79) – Tall, slim, athletic breed of horse used in racing and other equestrian sports.

Points of a Horse

1. poll
2. ear
3. eye
4. mane
5. crest
6. withers
7. back
8. loins
9. croup
10. dock
11. flank
12. tail
13. tendons
14. hock joint
15. stomach

16. elbow
17. heel
18. hoof
19. coronet band
20. pastern
21. fetlock joint
22. cannon bone
23. knee
24. shoulder
25. chin groove
26. nostril
27. muzzle
28. nose
29. cheekbone
30. forelock

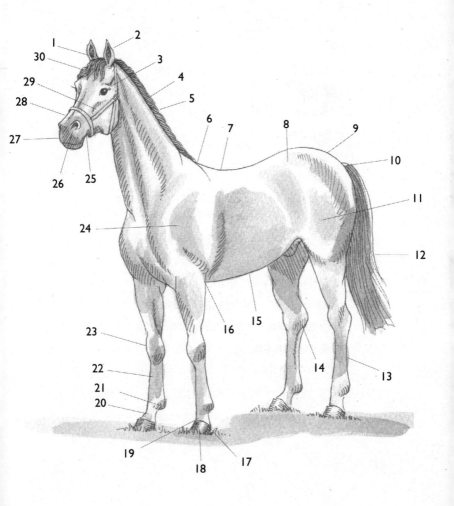

119

Pippa Funnell

*"Winning is amazing for a minute, but then
I am striving again to reach my next goal."*

I began learning to ride when I was six, on a little
pony called Pepsi.

When I was seven, I joined my local Pony Club –
the perfect place to learn more about riding and
caring for horses.

By the time I was fourteen and riding my first
horse, Sir Barnaby, my dream of being an event
rider was starting to take shape.

Two years later, I was offered the opportunity
to train as a working pupil in Norfolk with Ruth
McMullen, the legendary riding teacher. I jumped at
the chance.

In 1987, Sir Barnaby and I won the individual gold together at the Young Rider European Championships, which was held in Poland.

Since then, hard work and determination have taken me all the way to the biggest eventing competitions in the world. I've been lucky and had success at major events like Bramham, Burghley, Badminton, Luhmühlen, Le Lion d'Angers, Hickstead, Blenheim, Windsor, Saumur, Pau, Kentucky – and the list goes on...

I married William Funnell in 1993. William is an international show jumper and horse breeder. He has helped me enormously with my show jumping. We live on a farm in the beautiful Surrey countryside – with lots of stables!

Every sportsman or woman's wildest dream is to be asked to represent their country at the Olympics. So in 2000, when I was chosen for the Sydney Olympics, I was delighted. It was even more special to be part of the silver medal winning team.

Then, in 2003, I became the first (and only) person to win eventing's most coveted prize – the Rolex Grand Slam. The Grand Slam (winning three of the big events in a row – Badminton, Kentucky and Burghley) is the only three-day eventing slam in the sporting world.

2004 saw another Olympics and another call-up. Team GB performed brilliantly again and won another well-deserved silver medal, and I was lucky enough to win an individual bronze.

Having had several years without any top horses, I spent my time producing youngsters, so it was great in 2010 when one of those came through – Redesigned, a handsome chestnut gelding. In June that year I won my third Bramham International Horse Trials title on Redesigned. We even managed a clear show jumping round in the pouring rain! By the end of 2010, Redesigned was on the squad for the World Championships in Kentucky where we finished fifth.

Today, as well as a hectic competition schedule, I'm also busy training horses for the future. At the Billy Stud, I work with my husband, William, and top breeder, Donal Barnwell, to produce top-class sport horses.

And in between all that I love writing the *Tilly's Pony Tails* books, and I'm also a trustee of World Horse Welfare, a fantastic charity dedicated to giving abused and neglected horses a second chance in life. For more information, visit their website at www.worldhorsewelfare.org.

Acknowledgements

Three years ago when my autobiography was
published I never imagined that I would find myself
writing children's books. Huge thanks go to Louisa
Leaman for helping me to bring Tilly to life, and
to Jennifer Miles for her wonderful illustrations.

Many thanks to Fiona Kennedy for persuading and
encouraging me to search my imagination and for all her
hard work, along with the rest of the team at Orion.
Due to my riding commitments I am not the easiest
person to get hold of as my agent Jonathan Marks
at MTC has found. It's a relief he has been able
to work on all the agreements for me.

Much of my thinking about Tilly has been done
out loud in front of family, friends and godchildren –
thank you all for listening.

More than anything I have to acknowledge my four-legged
friends – my horses. It is thanks to them, and the
great moments I have had with them, that I was able to
create a girl, Tilly, who like me follows her passions.

Pippa Funnell
Forest Green, February 2009

For more about Tilly and
Silver Shoe Farm – including pony tips,
quizzes and everything you ever wanted
to know about horses –
visit www.tillysponytails.co.uk

Look out for

Pippa Funnell: Follow Your Dreams

Pippa Funnell as you've never seen her before.

Get to know Pippa – her loves, her hates, her friends,
her family. Meet her beautiful horses, and take a sneaky peek
at life on her gorgeous farm. Find out how she prepares
for important competitions, trains and cares for her horses, and
still has the time to write *Tilly's Pony Tails*.

And discover how, with hard work, passion and
determination, you too can follow your dreams,
just like Pippa.

978 1 4440 0266 9

£6.99